Max's New Baby

Danielle Steel
Max's New Baby

Illustrated by Jacqueline Rogers

Delacorte Press

Published by
Delacorte Press
Bantam Doubleday Dell Publishing Group, Inc.
666 Fifth Avenue
New York, New York 10103

Library of Congress Cataloging in Publication Data

Steel, Danielle.
Max's new baby / by Danielle Steel ; illustrated by Jacqueline Rogers.
p.   cm.
Summary: Unsure about the prospect of having a new baby in the house, four-and-a-half-year-old Max finally decides that it might not be so bad after all.
ISBN 0-385-29798-X
[1. Babies—Fiction. 2. Brothers and sisters—Fiction. 3. Family life—Fiction.] I. Rogers, Jacqueline, ill. II. Title.
PZ7.S8143Maxo   1989
[E]—dc19   88-35251
                                                         CIP
                                                          AC

design by Judith Neuman-Cantor
Manufactured in the United States of America

November 1989

10 9 8 7 6 5 4 3 2 1

To Zara, the littlest, newest sweet precious baby.

With all my love,
Mommy

This is Max. Max's Daddy is a fireman
and his Mommy is a nurse. They live in
New York.

Max's Daddy got a medal for bravery once. He saved two little girls and a baby in a hotel fire. Max's Mommy works in a hospital nursery, where they take care of brand-new babies. Max has visited his Mommy there lots of times. The babies are very little.

When Max was four and a half years old, his Mommy and Daddy told him they had a surprise for him. He wondered if it was going to be a new bicycle. Or maybe even a new car, which his Mommy said they needed. Or roller skates, which he wanted for his birthday. His birthday was in August. Max thought new roller skates would be terrific.

"No," his Daddy explained. "It's not anything like that. It's something even better." Better than roller skates? It was hard to imagine what that would be.

Max's Mommy was smiling. "It's a wonderful surprise, sweetheart. We're having a baby. In August, right around your birthday."

"You are?" Max was very surprised. He wasn't sure a new baby was such a great birthday gift after all. He liked being by himself with his Mommy and Daddy. Babies were cute in the hospital. But what would a baby be like at home? His friend Steven had one, and his was pretty messy.

It spat up a lot. It gooped food all over its face at dinnertime. It wore diapers and sometimes made a mess everywhere. You couldn't even play with it, because if you got too rough it cried, and Steven's Mom yelled. In fact, Steven's baby was no fun at all. Max couldn't see any reason why his would be either.

"Aren't you happy, Max?" Max's Mommy looked disappointed. He tried to sound happy for her, but he really wasn't. The more he thought about it, the more worried he got. This was going to be difficult, this business of having a new baby. Where would it sleep? What would it play with?

"Is it a boy or a girl?" Max asked. If it was a boy, it might try to take his Yankees catcher's mitt. That really would be awful.

"We don't know what it is yet." Max's Mommy smiled at him. "We might find out later, if we get something called a sonogram. But we might not need to do that. A sonogram is a picture of the baby inside my tummy. Sometimes they can see if the baby is a boy or a girl. They can see other things, too, like how many fingers and toes it has, and if it's all right and everything looks normal."

"Oh," Max said. He still wasn't happy. If it was a girl, it would probably cry all the time like his friend Andrew's baby sister.

She was a pest. But if it was a boy, he might want Max's new remote-controlled tractor. He could tell this was going to be a serious problem.

    As time went on, Max's Mommy
started to get fat. Well, not fat really,
just round, in the tummy.
    By Easter, Max's Mommy looked pretty
big to him. In the summer, at their
Fourth of July picnic, her tummy looked
really enormous. They still didn't know
if it was a girl or a boy. Max didn't really
care. He knew that whatever it would
be, it was going to be a problem.

It already was. For four and a half, almost five, years, Max had had a playroom and a bedroom. Now, suddenly, there was no more playroom. He had to play in their big, cozy kitchen, or the living room, or the little garden. The playroom was gone forever. It was going to belong to the baby.

His Daddy had painted it white. There were pink and blue and white baby things all over the room. It looked pretty, but Max missed his playroom.

They didn't know the baby's name yet either. It was going to be Sam if it was a boy, and Charlotte if it was a girl. Max had already decided that if it was a girl, he'd call her Charlie.

    After the Fourth of July picnic, Max's Mommy didn't want to go anywhere. It was hot. Max's mother said she just couldn't move. So Max was especially happy when his Daddy took some time off and took him out whenever he could. But he also had to stay home with Max's Mommy. It wasn't nice to leave her alone now, right before the baby. It could come at any minute. Max was just hoping it didn't come on his birthday. It was bad enough as it was. He had to share his parents and his house. He'd lost his playroom, his old crib, which he still loved, his high chair, his stroller, and some teddy bears his Mommy said she was sure he'd want to give to the baby now. But he really didn't— and he certainly didn't want to share his birthday too. That was just asking too much! He hoped that the baby would come before or after.

As it turned out, the baby *didn't* come on Max's birthday. He had a wonderful fifth birthday party. His Mommy baked a special cake for him and he even got his roller skates. But still no baby sister or brother.

Two weeks later, on a Saturday afternoon, near the end of August, Max's Daddy had some news. They were going to take Max to Jean, his baby-sitter. He was going to stay there until Mommy had the baby. Daddy didn't think it would be more than a few hours.

Max's suitcase was already packed, just as Mommy's was for the hospital. She was very quiet on the way to Jean's. Max's Daddy kept asking her how she felt. All of a sudden Max felt very excited. He'd been waiting for this baby for so long that now he wanted to know who this baby was. Was it a boy or a girl? What did it look like?

Max's Mommy gave him an extra big hug when they got to Jean's house. She looked him right in the eye and told him that he was always going to be her special boy. And she told him how much she loved him. "The baby won't change anything, sweetheart. I'll always, always love you." He felt better after that.

Max and Jean waved as they drove away.
Daddy promised he'd call as soon as
the baby came.

Jean suggested they make cookies
and lemonade while they waited. They
were delicious. But the phone still hadn't
rung when they finished.

Then they made dinner. Jean cooked hamburgers and spinach and french fries. They had cupcakes for dessert and still Max's Daddy didn't call. Jean made popcorn. They colored in a new coloring book she had bought. Then *finally,* the phone rang.

"Guess what!" Max's Daddy said as soon as Jean handed the phone to Max with a big smile.

"Is it a girl or a boy?" Max asked.

"Which one did you want?" Max's Daddy sounded very happy.

"Umm . . ." Max still wasn't sure if he wanted a sister or a brother. "A sister," he said. Then he changed his mind. "No, a brother."

"Then in that case"—Max's Daddy laughed —"you got what you wanted."

"I did? It's a brother?" All of a sudden that sounded good to Max. A brother would play baseball with him one day, and football, and tag. And they could go roller-skating together.

"Mommy's fine." Daddy sounded very happy. "And you have a baby brother named Sam. He weighs seven pounds. He looks a lot like you did."

"He does?" All of a sudden Max felt proud to be a big brother. "Can I see him?"

"You sure can. First thing tomorrow morning. I'll come to get you at Jean's. But first, I have another surprise for you."

Daddy was laughing again, and so was
Max. Sam. A boy. A baby brother!
Suddenly all Max's worries about him
over the past months didn't seem very
important.

"What's the other surprise, Dad?"

"You also have a baby sister named
Charlotte. Mommy had twins, and no
one knew she was going to. They were
hiding behind each other in Mommy's
tummy."

"They were?" Max looked amazed.
"Wow! A sister too! Sam *and* Charlie . . . !"

"Max and Sam and Charlie." His Daddy
corrected him. "She weighed six and a
half pounds and wait till you see her.
She's really pretty! She looks just like
Mommy."

As soon as Max got off the phone he
told Jean all about it, and she was
excited too. Twins were really special.

When Max saw the twins the next day, he couldn't decide which one was cuter. His Daddy took pictures of everyone. His Mommy was so happy to see Max, she almost cried. It was a happy day for all of them.

Now Max didn't even mind giving up
his playroom. Sam and Charlie were
really going to need it!